Neah's Escape Copy

Mission #1 Neah Does It Her Way

Latoya Panton

Illustrations by Jago Panton

Book 1 edition 2025

ISBN: 979-8-9907144-2-7

This book is dedicated to my wonderful students whom
I have had the privilege of teaching over the span of
two-decades. You have truly been my inspiration. And to my
two beautiful boys, who were my number one critics. This
could not have been possible without you. Keep reading
guys.

Neah is the brave and determined heart of the team. She's curious, bold, and always willing to face danger head-on—especially when her friends are in trouble. As the main protagonist, Neah's role is to lead the group through mysterious missions and monster-filled challenges.

Gina is Neah's fearless and loyal best friend. While Neah is bold and adventurous, Gina is the strategist—quick-thinking, calm under pressure, and always ready with a plan. She supports Neah by keeping her grounded, reminding her of their mission when emotions run high, and using her magic-watch and waist pack to track enemies, unlock clues, or deploy gadgets when needed.

Alex is Neah's 13-year-old older brother—a tech-savvy, fearless adventurer with a strong protective instinct. Dressed in sleek gear and piloting his own high-tech spacecraft, Alex plays a vital support role as the team's rescuer and tactical lead during the most dangerous missions.

Worn with pride and purpose, the backpack carries not only Neah books and supplies but also her most treasured items, including her grandmother's necklace and hidden notes she scribbles in moments of reflection.

The emerald stone is a mysterious and powerful gem embedded in Neah's necklace. Gifted to her by her grandmother, the stone glows softly in times of danger, offering warmth, protection, and guidance. It is believed to be ancient, holding secrets that connect Neah to a hidden legacy and a force greater than she ever imagined. As the series unfolds, the emerald becomes a key to unlocking paths, revealing truths, and helping Neah overcome the darkness she and her friends must face.

Though it looks simple at first glance, Gina's wristwatch is one of her most powerful tools on every mission. A small button on the side unlocks its power to briefly freeze time or reveal hidden messages.

Journey with Neah on her other adventures

Discover Your World

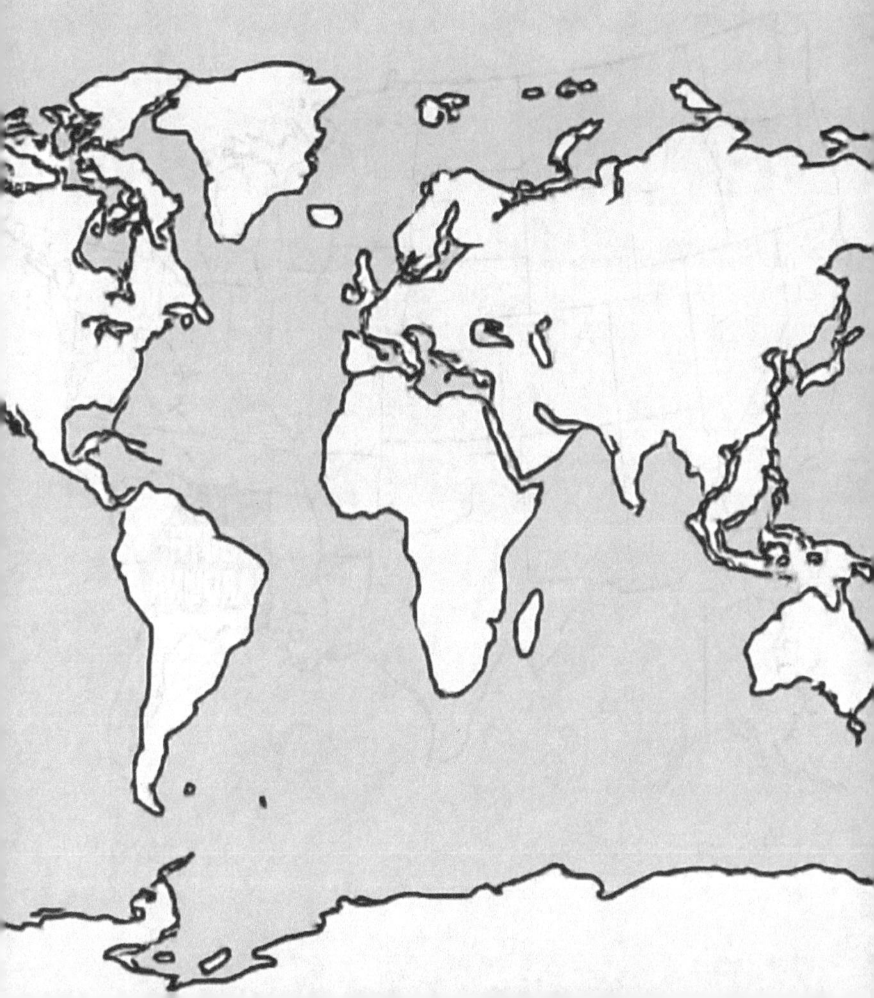

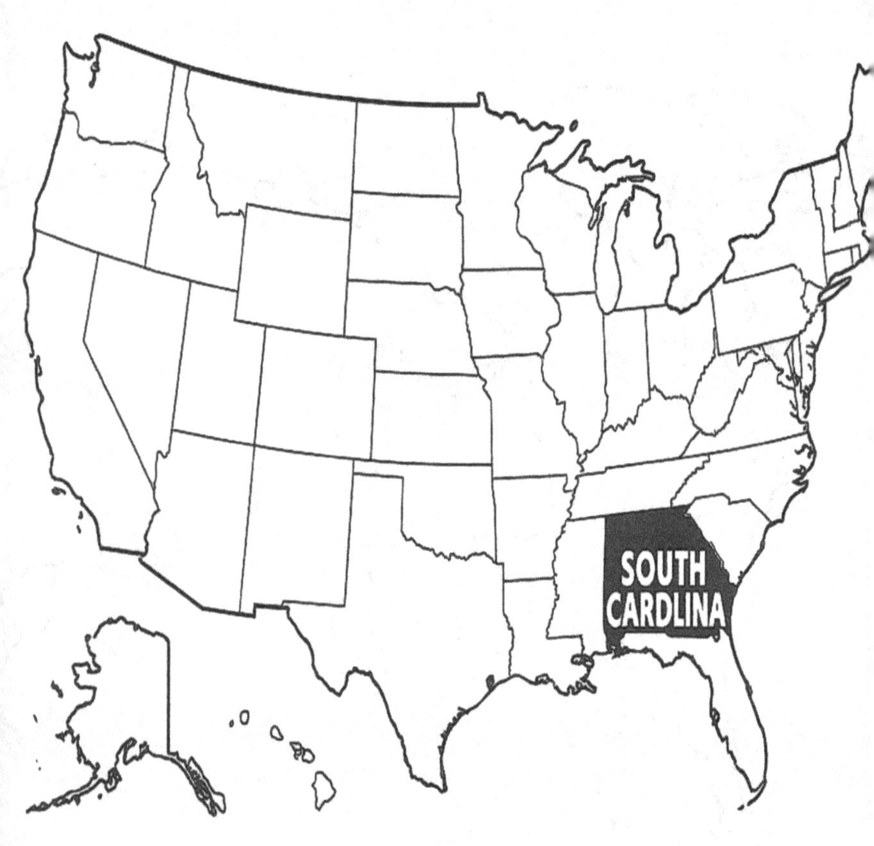

SOUTH
CARDLINA

Contents

Chapter 1

School Sucks

Neah received a sharp slap on her cheek from the winter's breeze as she stepped out of her house on Albany Lane, headed for school. It was one of the harshest winters she had experienced since moving to the U.S. three years ago. In fact, it was the first time Columbia had seen snow since 1880—and Neah was not fond of it.

Furthermore, it was freezing on her way to the car, and Neah struggled to reach her gloves tucked into the side pocket of her backpack. She glanced toward the light coming from her mom's car as she reached for the items she had hidden there.

As she trudged along the narrow path toward the car, Neah hissed and mumbled to herself. Her feet struggled through the 3.5 inches of snow that encircled her doorway and stretched all the way to the gate.

"Hurry, Neah! We're going to be late for school," called her mother.

Neah rushed forward and gripped the handle of the open car door, exhaling warm breaths to push back the biting cold air.

Soon, she settled herself in the back seat and curled up under the new pink and white blanket her mom had bought for her weeks earlier. From the front seat, her mother glanced back and asked gently, "Are you okay back there?"

"I'm fine," Neah muttered.

As her mom backed out of the driveway and headed toward the exit of their apartment complex, Neah's stomach twisted. Just the thought of going to school made her feel sick. Oh, how she dreaded that place. The kids there teased her every word and mocked her accent.

"School sucks!" Neah burst out from behind her mom's seat.

"Don't say that!" her mother gushed. "In no time, you will have many friends," she insisted with hopeful reassurance.

Neah wished she could find a way to escape back to her homeland—Jamaica. The land of wood and water. The place where the glorious blue waves kiss the horizon beneath skies of majestic beauty. Where the warmth of the sun ignites your mind, body, and soul. Where the soul-filled music snakes its way into your spirit, leaving you dazed and inspired to become the best version of yourself.

And oh, the people. Their electrifying smiles and warm embraces could melt even the coldest heart, making you feel like family.

Neah thought about asking her mom to let her visit her grandparents in Jamaica for the summer. Maybe, just maybe, Grammy could convince her mom to let her stay. But summer was still months away, and for now, Neah would have to wait—and quietly hold on to her plan.

Chapter 2

Thinking About Home

"Yum, yum!" she thought, relishing the idea of this delicious meal.

Oh, how she longed to see her Grammy again. But summer was months away, and Neah would have to wait a while before seeing her Grams again. At least she had the special silver necklace Grammy had given her on her last visit.

A smile trickled across her face as she remembered Grammy's words:

"This is my special little gift to you, my child. Whenever you feel sad, just know I am right there with you," Grammy had said, placing the necklace gently around her neck.

From early on, Neah knew there was something special about the necklace. It had a metallic finish with several interlocking links and a shiny red emerald stone set in a silver aluminum pendant. Whenever it caught the sunlight, it glistened with a magical glow.

As Neah caressed the necklace between her tiny fingers, she reminisced about the delicious meals Grammy used to cook. Grammy was known far and wide for her tantalizing cooking skills. Strangely though, despite never eating chicken herself, she cooked it better than anyone else Neah knew.

One memory came crashing down on her like an avalanche—the time Grammy cooked Neah's favorite hen.

The chicken, affectionately named **Jean**, had been a gift to Neah and was her most prized possession. In fact, every one of Grammy's grandchildren had been given a hen. It was a cherished tradition whenever they came to spend the summer.

But this time, Neah was not delighted. Jean was to be the *sacrificed lamb* for Sunday dinner. Tim and Beth, her cousins, had their hens cooked weeks earlier. There was no backing out now. Grammy had warned them all: if she ran out of money, the hens would be used for food.

Felisha and Jessa, the other two hens, had already met their end. Now it was Jean's turn.

The morning had come. The sun rose in a majestic blue sky over the breadfruit and pear trees facing the house. Grammy had been announcing since the last kill that Neah's chicken was next—especially after the tangerine sale to a local merchant had fallen through.

Neah watched silently from a distance as Grammy walked toward the chicken coop. She secured Jean by the wings in her firm grip. Neah felt like all the breath had left her body when she saw her pet hanging helplessly in Grammy's hands.

As was custom, the chicken would be tied by the feet to a branch, its head hanging down.

Neah began to cry.

"Grammy, yu a go kill mi Jeanie?"

"Yes," Grammy replied from under the tangerine tree.

"Remember, if we don't kill this chicken, you and your cousins won't have any dinner."

Neah wilted. She dreaded the thought of seeing her only pet slaughtered.

Tim and Beth gathered at the brow of the hill to witness Jean's final moments.

"Hey Neah, ready for some chicken wings?" Tim teased.

"I want dem chicken legs," chuckled Beth.

Neah's face wrinkled with fury. She stormed up the stairs and buried her head under her pillow, trying to block out the terrifying sounds of Jean's flapping wings as Grammy butchered her.

"Neah! Neah! Come look—Jean is dead!" cried Tim.

Neah reluctantly pulled herself off the bed and went to see what was left. There, she saw Jean lying headless in a bucket of water mixed with lemon and vinegar. A somber mood overtook her.

"Well, life goes on," Beth shrugged.

"You knew Grammy was going to kill your hen one day. Get over it."

Bruised by the loss, Neah disappeared to the back of the

house, unable to think of a way to escape the misery. Eventually, she eased herself back under her blanket, gazing at the longleaf pine trees standing like rear guards along the road. Their needle-like leaves, growing in bunches, reminded her of the warmth and unity of her community back in Jamaica.

Neah relaxed in the back seat of the car as her mom's favorite song came on the radio.

"Won't He do it? I know He will!" her mom sang, buckling her seatbelt and turning toward Neah's school.

Meanwhile, Neah drifted into her favorite place—**Jamaica**. It was the place she had called home all her life, and that wasn't going to change anytime soon.

Her mind wandered back to her elementary school days when she and her friends would play **Dandy Shandy** in the open field. Day after day, they would sneak away during lunch to play. The game, invented in Jamaica in the 1950s, was mainly played by girls and had become a beloved pastime.

Neah's face lit up as she remembered one round with her friends **Longie** and **Nye**. It was her turn to dodge the ball while they threw. With her athletic skills, Neah could dodge expertly, even hoisting her left leg up to a near 180-degree angle. She darted between her friends and leapt over a little cardboard box stuffed with paper—her own kind of victory. She felt unstoppable.

Chapter 3

Let's Play

Like Jackie Robinson stepping up to home plate, Longie stepped out with the little carton ball vibrating with energy in her hands. She secured her feet in position and swung her hand in the air, ready to launch the ball.

As the sun glared down on her between the trees, she

winked at Nye before releasing it.

The ball, which seemed to be flying at 80 km/h, zoomed across Neah's chest, nearly knocking her to the ground.

Neah knew she would have to step up her game if she wanted to win the bet.

The three girls had made a deal: whoever scored ten points first would receive twenty dollars from the other two players.

At this point, Neah was down by seven points, meaning she only needed three more to win. Trying to prevent her from scoring, Longie and Nye concocted a sneaky plan—to throw a bait ball over Neah's head.

First, Longie tossed a non-threatening ball to Nye, giving her just enough time to make a move. As Neah moved in closer, Nye caught the ball, steadied her stance, and with a swift motion, released it.

WHACK!

The ball struck Neah right on her buttocks, sending her tumbling to the ground.

"Awww!!" cried Neah, clutching her backside, trying to squeeze away the sting of the impact.

"Gottahyuh!" Nye hollered from the pitch.

With a grin of satisfaction zigzagging across Neah's full

lips, she launched into another fond memory of her and her best friend, Trom.

Like Trom, Neah's mom worked in the city most of the year, so she had to stay with her grandmother in the country. The cool hills of Manchester were where they forged a never-ending friendship.

Neah's mind suddenly raced back as she heard her mom calling,

"Neah! Neah! Are you alright back there?"

"Yes," Neah answered as she jolted forward, trying to regain her balance from the sudden jerk of the car.

"I was just asking you what you wanted for dinner later," her mother said, keeping a steady rock to the music playing in the background.

"I don't know... maybe pizza," Neah responded.

With only a few meters left before they arrived at school, Neah escaped back to her favorite place—her imagination—to get one last bit of satisfaction before stepping out for the day.

Where was I? she asked herself, searching her thoughts for the spot she had left off before her mother's interruption.

With her head tilted back, her mind recalled the taste of

fried dumplings, ripe plantains, and salt mackerel—just the way Grammy always prepared them.

Chapter 4

Getting Over Jean

For hours, Neah sat sobbing over her pet hen, Jean, as she remembered the first day they met. It felt like just yesterday. Jean had the most beautiful brown and white feathers that seemed to glisten in the sunlight when she walked. She was also very plump, which made her the cutest little hen in the yard.

Oh well, Neah thought. *I guess this is where we have to part ways.*

No more clucking at the sound of rodents trespassing in the yard.

No more beautiful brown eggs, laid so neatly in the chicken coop for her to collect after school.

No more majestic walks around the yard.

Neah wiped her eyes, thinking about her sweet pet hen.

When Sunday came and Grammy called the children for dinner, Neah retreated to her hiding spot in the back of the yard. Her heart raced a hundred miles per minute.

She dreaded the thought of eating her for dinner.

Sure, she was hungry—but who eats their pet for dinner?

No matter what the situation is, Neah told herself, *no matter how hard life gets, eating one's pet should never be an option.*

She paced back and forth, crafting a plan to explain her absence from the dinner table.

I could tell her I have a tummy ache and can't eat... or better yet, I'll say I'm allergic to chicken!

As the plan settled in her mind, Neah felt a sudden sense of peace.

That's it. I'll say I get allergies from eating chicken, she decided.

"Neah! Neah!" Grammy called from the outdoor kitchen. "Come have your dinner!"

Neah's heart fluttered again.

"Coming, Ma!" she shouted from the main house.

She knew she would have to muster up all the courage she had to convince Grammy that she didn't like chicken anymore—because of *allergies*.

But how could she explain the many times she had devoured a warm plate of curried chicken and rice? Or stew chicken with green bananas? Not to mention the chicken foot soup Grammy made on Saturday afternoons. That soup was *finger-licking good*.

It was as if Grammy had put her whole *foot* in that soup.

But now, Neah had to make a choice.

She loved Jean too much. Eating her pet was never an option.

Still, Neah knew Grammy didn't play the *"I'm not hungry"* game. As far as Grammy was concerned, kids had two choices:

Eat and live, or don't eat and get a whooping.

Neah slowly exited the house and walked gingerly up the steps to the outdoor kitchen that sat on top of the little hill in the yard.

As she got closer, she noticed some kittens playing in a nest of bushes beside the kitchen. She paused to watch them pounce and tumble. Then she spotted a cluster of *touch-me-nots* in the grass.

Wait a minute, Neah thought. *Let me go check these out.*

She loved pressing her fingers against the plants and watching them magically fold in.

"Neah, where are you?" Grammy called again.

"I'm coming, Grammy!" Neah answered, only a few steps away from the kitchen door.

Tim and Beth had already secured their spots in the wooden kitchen and were licking their fingers as they devoured their meal—curried chicken legs.

Neah could smell the strong scent of Jean's cooked body seeping through the cracks in the wooden walls. The aroma was soaked in familiar spices—onions, garlic, thyme, and pimento—just the way Grammy marinated all her meats.

"Here. Come sit down," Tim said.

"Your dinner is over there," Grammy added, pointing to a small red plate at the end of the table.

Neah's stomach turned at the sight of Jean's chopped-up body.

To Tim and Beth, it was a tasty meal.

But to Neah, it was the butchered remains of her beloved pet.

How barbaric, she thought. *Who kills their pet and eats it for dinner?*

She sat and stared in disbelief, unable to lift her fork.

With a dozen unanswered questions spinning through her mind, she knew one thing for sure—she would never look at her Grammy the same way again.

Her beautiful, sweet Grammy...

Had turned into a *witch*—a witch who killed her pet.

And she could never trust her cousins, Tim and Beth. If they could eat Jean, they could do *anything.*

I have to find a way to escape this place, Neah thought. *These people are monsters.*

And who knows... they might want to eat me next.

Neah eased herself back into the chair, holding in the scream that was rising inside her.

Chapter 5

Honoring Jean

Meanwhile, Grammy came in with the drinks.

"Hey Neah, are you going to eat?" she asked.

"No, Grammy. I'm not feeling hungry at all. In fact, my stomach has been aching for some time now."

"Oh no! I wonder if you're coming down with the stomach bug," Grammy said, searching Neah's eyes.

"Well, maybe. You know a lot of kids have been getting sick lately," Neah replied.

"Sure thing. I'll just make you some fresh mint tea. That should calm your stomach down a bit. Would you like some tea, Neah?" Grammy asked.

"Definitely! That would be great."

Neah sighed in relief. *Thank goodness I don't have to eat my wonderful pet. How could I ever do such a thing?*

But something felt strange. *Grammy wasn't angry at all,* Neah thought. *In fact, she was so calm when I told her I wasn't hungry.*

Well, I don't care—as long as I don't have to eat my pet, I'm perfectly fine, Neah whispered under her breath.

Meanwhile, Tim and Beth were having the time of their lives—making jokes and licking their fingertips as they gushed over how delicious the meal was.

Neah hurriedly drank her cup of mint tea and asked to be excused from the dinner table.

"Can I go to bed now, Grammy?" Neah asked. "I want to go to bed."

"Sure," Grammy said. "Make sure you say your prayers

before you go to sleep," she added as Neah vanished out of sight into the house.

Neah dashed inside, feeling a sense of relief that she had done the right thing. She had kept her loyalty to her hen, and that was all that mattered.

Neah quickly washed up, put on her favorite pink and white nightdress, and went to bed.

Chapter 6

Getting A Dog For My Pet

As Neah pulled the covers over her head, she whispered the prayer her Grammy always made her say:

In my little bed I lie:

Heavenly Father, hear my cry;

If I should die before I wake,

I pray Thee, Lord, my soul to take.

That night, Neah dreamt of Jean—taking her usual majestic strides around the house and making her familiar clucking sounds as she chased rodents in the yard.

Neah tried to get close to her, but every time she came near, Jean would dodge her and disappear into the distance. It was as though they were playing a game of hide and seek.

As soon as Neah got close, Jean would run up the hill, then down again, clucking with pride.

"Okay, Jean. You win," Neah said, almost exhausted.

It sure is hard having a chicken for a pet, she thought to herself.

Soon the night was over, and the sun came peeking through the window.

"Wake up, guys!" Grammy called from the other room. "Remember, we have to go visit Aunty Joan at the market today!"

Aunty Joan made some of the most delicious bammys—soft and chewy. And every summer, Grammy always made sure they had some to take back home for Mom and the neighbors.

Neah twisted and turned in the bed, trying to get a few more minutes in her warm, cozy blanket.

Scenes from her dream of Jean flashed through her mind.

Well, I guess Jean is happy after all, Neah thought.

It really is hard having a chicken for a pet. All my friends have dogs, cats, or hamsters. Why did I have to get a chicken?

"This time, I'm going to ask Grams for a dog," Neah said to herself.

Furthermore, dogs are intelligent, friendly, and cuddly. You can hug them, play with them, and even pet them. And they certainly don't run away when you try to cuddle them.

That's it. I want a dog for my pet, Neah concluded.

As Neah and her cousins got dressed for the market, she thought about how she was going to break the news to Grammy—that she wanted a dog the next time she came to visit.

As Neah, Tim, and Beth made their way up the steep hill onto the road, Neah relished the thought of having a pet dog. The idea made her feel warm inside.

I can't wait, she thought, as visions of a nice little poodle—or maybe a German Shepherd—settled in her mind.

Chapter 7

Dealing With Melisa

As her mom made the final turn around the curve, Neah's body jerked forward at the sound of her mom's voice calling from outside the car door.

"Come on, let's go!" her mom called, standing by the car and handing Neah her backpack. "You need to hurry, or you're going to be late."

"Late for what?" Neah bellowed.

Looking out the door, her eyes caught sight of the other vehicles dropping off kids at the school entrance.

"NOT AGAIN!" Neah gushed in frustration. "Why do I even have to go to school? Why can't I just do my work at home?" she complained.

And furthermore, she thought, *that place is like a prison. You go inside those brick walls, the lady at the front hands you a bag with a lousy peanut butter sandwich, a musty apple, and a box of milk. If you're lucky, you might get a corn dog or a softly baked muffin. I wonder what I'll get today...* Neah grumbled to herself as she reluctantly crawled out of the car.

"Remember, honey plum, I can't leave you at home by yourself," her mom replied. "And I bet you'll have plenty of exciting activities at school," she added with a hopeful smile.

Neah hated the thought of going to school—but what she hated even more was Melisa, *The Wicked Wizard of Oz.*

Melisa earned that nickname because she made everyone's lives miserable. She was always complaining to the teacher that someone was picking on her—whether it was about her grassy-looking hair, her big, bulgy eyes, or the loud slurping sounds she made at the cafeteria table while eating spaghetti.

To make matters worse, she once told the teacher that Neah was staring at her during class, which made her uncomfortable. As a result, the teacher moved Neah from her seat and placed her all the way in the back of the classroom.

That made Neah furious. She had to fight the urge to yank Melisa's big, untidy ponytail right off the back of her head.

If I could just get her to myself for one minute, Neah fumed silently, *then she'd learn never to mess with me again.*

Chapter 8

Brave Steps

Neah made tiny steps toward the school doors of Bakers Elementary. Unlike her, the other kids seemed so excited to go into the building. Neah watched as one little girl gave her mom a kiss and jumped out of the car.

"Hey, Matty!" she called out to her friend, who was a few

steps ahead.

"Hi, Hailey," the friend responded. The two girls gave each other a light embrace and continued into the building.

Neah stood frozen for a few seconds.

I wish I were as happy as they were to go into this devastating place, Neah muttered, clutching the necklace around her neck.

The words of her grandmother came rushing back: *"Whenever you feel afraid, just think of me, my love. I'm right there with you."*

"Here, Neah," her mom said, giving her one last hug before leaving her at the front door.

Neah wanted to cry, but somehow, she managed to hold back the tears.

"You'll be fine, Neah. You'll be fine," she said aloud, trying to console her eleven-year-old mind. *At least you have Gina and Christian,* she thought to herself as she slowly trudged down the fifth-grade hallway.

And if that girl Melisa ever tries to tease me about my accent again, she will get what's coming to her, Neah threatened silently.

Soon, she entered the classroom and did a full 360-degree

scan of the room.

Where is Gina? Thoughts raced through her mind. *Oh, I see her—over there by the library. And Christian? Yeah, there he is, chatting it up with DJ and Joel. Today will be a good day,* Neah thought.

She quickly walked down to the cubbies, placed her bookbag inside, and pulled out her assignment for Mrs. Winters. That was everyone's usual routine when they got to class. Mrs. Winters was the meanest person when it came to homework. It was like she turned into some strange creature from outer space if you said you forgot it. Her eyes would become cold, the hair on the top of her head seemed to stand up, and her voice grew so coarse.

But once you handed her the homework, she treated you the sweetest. You could even expect to get something from her treasure chest of treats.

Still, that was the least of Neah's worries. Just getting through the day without Melisa messing with her was the ultimate goal.

And sure enough, Melisa was there—right up in the front row. Everyone knew she was the teacher's pet because she told on everybody... except her friend Judy.

Mrs.
WINTERS

Chapter 9

The Big Fight

Mrs. Winters got the class ready for their usual class meeting, where she had the students share how they spent their weekends. It was Neah's turn.

"Well, my weekend was great. I got to talk to my grandmother, and my mom, dad, and brother made jerk chicken,"

Neah said proudly.

"Jerk chicken? What's that?" Melisa asked, giggling.

Neah's countenance fell. Her eyes widened, and her lips folded in disappointment.

Meanwhile, Christian and Gina could sense the rage building inside her.

"Take it easy, Neah. Don't let that girl get to you. She ain't worth it," Gina whispered, trying to comfort her.

"Yeah," Mrs. Winters chimed in. "That's not even a nice thing to say, Melisa. In fact, jerk chicken is one of my favorite foods. You should try some one day."

"Yes, dummy, you should try it," Christian muttered under his breath, clearly annoyed.

Mrs. Winters ended the class meeting, and everyone returned to their seats.

See, this is why I don't want to come to school. I'm sick of them teasing me about my culture, my accent, and my people, Neah muttered under her breath.

"It's okay, Neah. I got you," Gina said. "You'll be fine. And by the way, I love your culture, your food, and your people. Don't listen to Melisa—she's just jealous, that's all"

The two girls giggled as they made their way back to their

seats.

A few minutes later, when Neah went to sharpen her pencil at the back table, Melisa appeared right beside her.

"Get away from me, you gorilla," Neah snapped.

Gina and Christian, sitting nearby, could see how aggravated Neah had become. It was as if a forest fire had swept into the classroom, burning red-hot between the two girls.

Soon, Neah and Melisa's eyes collided like two airplanes in midair. Gina and Christian knew it—Neah was about to strike.

"Neah!" Gina called from across the room. "She ain't worth it, girl. Let it go!"

"Definitely not," Christian added, nodding in support.

But as the hairs on the back of Neah's neck stood up, there was no turning back. Today was the day Neah would redefine herself—the day no one would dare mess with her again.

Meanwhile, Mrs. Winters had stepped next door to keep an eye on Miss Spence's class while she took a restroom break. With one eye on the other room and one eye flicking back to her own, Neah knew this was her moment to strike.

Gina and Christian gave Neah the cut-throat signal to

back off—but Neah was in too deep.

Ever since Melisa's last complaint got her moved to the back of the class, Neah had made up her mind: she was going to teach Melisa a solid lesson.

"Okay. Say one more word to me, you oversized Chihuahua," Neah muttered under her breath. *I'll teach you a lesson you'll never forget.*

"You're the Chihuahua," Melisa fired back.

"Keep running that mouth," Neah warned. She glanced toward Miss Winters and saw her attention still fixed on the other classroom.

Neah moved in closer.

"One more word from you, you little moron, and I'll twist your head off your body," she threatened.

"I'm not afraid of you," Melisa said in her small, mouse-like voice. "And by the way, you can't make me do anything, you coward."

That was the last straw.

Neah dropped her pencils. Within a flash, her small, five-inch fists shot toward Melisa's head. She grabbed her bushy ponytail and began spinning her around like a blade caught in a whirlpool.

"Ahhh! Let go of my hair, you oversized cockroach!" Melisa shrieked.

That made Neah even more furious. She sank her skinny little fingers deeper into the knot of Melisa's hair and pulled her toward the trash can.

"Fight! Fight! Fight!" the class chanted in unison.

Neah pushed Melisa's head deeper and deeper into the trash can.

Melisa's face turned hot pink as she struggled to push Neah off.

"Let go of me!" she cried desperately.

"You messed with the wrong one this time," Neah snapped. "I'm going to make you pay, you little worm."

"Keep my name outta your mouth, you green lizard," Neah growled.

Just then, Mrs. Winters rushed in and jumped between the girls.

"What do you girls think you're doing?" she shouted, struggling to pull them apart. "I hope you know you're both in big trouble!"

Mrs. Winters finally yanked Neah's hand out of Melisa's

hair. Neah still tried to get in a few more punches, but Mrs. Winters radioed the front office for reinforcement.

Within seconds, Mr. Bean came charging in.

"You two—again?" he sighed, clearly frustrated, as he marched them off to his office.

"Now the rest of you—quiet and back to work!" he commanded.

"Yes, Mr. Bean," the class replied in unison.

The room grew quiet again, though whispers and excited buzz filled the air.

Neah and Melisa's fight was now the hottest topic in school.

Chapter 10

Both Sides of The Story

Both girls were brought to the office, and Mr. Bean began his usual round of questions in a *Judge Judy*-style setting. He sat the girls in front of him and stared them square in the face.

"So, who started the fight?" Mr. Bean began, looking in

the direction of Neah.

"She did," both girls said at the same time, pointing to each other.

"Okay, calm down. Neah, what happened?" Mr. Bean asked, trying to gain some control of the conversation.

"Well, you see... what had happened was..." Neah stuttered before finally getting the words out. "Melissa had been spreading false rumors that I was calling her names and lying, saying I told Gina how her head was as big as a crater. And that Judy told her I said she didn't smell right. And Jerry said he heard me say her eyes were big and bulgy. And that wasn't true!"

She paused. "Well, even though we can all agree they *are* huge and bulgy, I didn't call her any names."

"Yes, you did!" Melissa fired back.

"Whew—hold up," Mr. Bean sighed, raising a hand to stop the back-and-forth before turning to Melissa.

"Now, Melissa, what happened?" Mr. Bean asked, looking at her.

"You see, Mr. Bean," Melissa said, "Neah and her friends always ignore me when I want to play with them."

Her voice grew softer as she continued. "They never let me

play on the playground, and they're always pushing me out of the group." Her voice cracked, and tears began trickling down her red cheeks.

"Here she goes crying again. Pitiful. Just pitiful," Neah mumbled.

"Is that true, Neah?" Mr. Bean asked, shifting his gaze toward her.

"No, it's not," Neah said with a slight smirk. "Well... kind of."

"She's just not like us, Mr. Bean. She's different. And she acts nerdy sometimes," Neah continued.

Mr. Bean leaned forward.

"No, Neah. You have to learn to be more kind. Melissa actually wants to be your friend, but you have to be a little more nice to her."

"Nice? I don't know how to do that," Neah said, throwing her hands up. "She needs to be a little tougher. She's always complaining about stuff."

"Okay, problem solved," Mr. Bean said, leaning back in his chair. "From now on, Neah—you'll be a little nicer. And Melissa—you'll be a little tougher. Deal?"

"Sure," Neah said.

"Yes," Melissa agreed.

"Now," Mr. Bean continued, "both of you will be suspended for five days."

The girls' mouths dropped.

"Go get your bags while I call your parents," Mr. Bean said with finality.

Chapter 11

Leaving Is Never Easy

Within minutes, Neah was summoned to the front office by Mrs. Burrowers, the lady who worked at the front desk.

"Neah, your mom is here!" Mrs. Burrowers called out.

Neah gingerly got up and walked to the cubbies to grab

her bookbag.

"Come on, Neah," Miss Winters said. "Don't keep your mom waiting."

Christian and Gina looked over at Neah with sadness in their eyes. They knew she was in big trouble—and that she was probably going to be grounded for the entire weekend.

The last time Neah got grounded for fighting at school, she missed Gina's birthday party and had to skip meeting Christian at the park for their usual game of soccer.

Neah leaned over to give Christian and Gina one last goodbye hug before walking out of the classroom.

"I'll call you!" Gina shouted from the back seat as Neah walked out the door.

As Neah walked along the hallway toward the front office, all she could do was clutch her good luck necklace—the one her grandmother gave her. Somehow, she felt warm inside whenever she held it. It was as if it had the power to make her forget all the chaos she was going through at that moment.

Then she remembered the words her Grammy had said:

"Whenever you feel afraid, just think of me, my love. I'm right there with you."

"Oh, how I wish you were here, Grammy," Neah whispered to herself as she turned the corner to the front office.

Back in the classroom, a massive cloud of sadness hung over the room as the rest of the class tried to come to terms with what had just happened.

Meanwhile, Melisa was getting ready to go home too—because, like Neah, her mom had been called to pick her up.

Melisa was the quietest she had ever been. Normally, she'd be chatting with her friend Judy, but now she sat in ghostly silence.

What in the world just happened? Melisa thought to herself as she moved toward the cubby to gather her things.

Seconds later, the call came in over the intercom.

"Early dismissal for Melisa Brady."

"Let's go," Miss Winters said hurriedly, directing Melisa to get all her stuff from the cubbies.

"Do you have all your books?" Miss Winters inquired. "And be sure to take home your science fair board. I'll be decluttering this weekend, so if you need your project, it's best to go get it now."

By this time, Melisa's face was blank, mixed with a bit of sadness and shock.

The whole class watched as Melisa piled everything up in her hands and tried to walk out the door. Realizing that it would be nearly impossible to carry it all, Miss Winters offered her a trash bag.

"Here, Melisa. Put the stuff in this bag," Miss Winters suggested.

Everyone was relieved as Melisa unloaded the books and projects into the white trash bag.

As she walked toward the classroom door, she took one last look at her classmates, trying to capture the fun moments she'd shared with them.

Her eyes landed on the math displays at the back table. Her project was one of the best—she had built a pyramid on *the powers of 10*. That project earned her a perfect score, and Melisa had been thrilled.

Next, she remembered her ELA argument essay—the one she had turned in late, but still received a good grade on.

Melisa fought with every fiber in her body to hold back the tears, but she couldn't.

One last look around the room at the familiar, friendly faces was just enough to push her over the edge. Tears streamed down her cheeks.

Miss Winters fought hard to push back her own emotions as well.

"You will be fine, Melisa. In no time, you'll be back at school with your friends," Miss Winters said, trying to console her.

Judy sobbed silently as Melisa said her last goodbyes.

"I'm going to miss you guys!" she cried before walking off.

What would life be like without Neah and Melisa? Gina wondered.

The thought of not seeing them for an entire week felt unreal.

Even though Melisa could be like an annoying little mosquito at times—and she got on everyone's nerves—life without her was going to be boring.

No more:

"Miss Winters, Neah and Gina don't want me to play with them!"

And no more:

"Leave me alone! You oversized cockroach," she would growl when provoked by Neah or the other kids.

ELISSA
Years Old

Chapter 12

Making Amends

Neah and Melisa arrived just in time to see their moms greeting each other in the parking lot.

"Hey, Ericka, what's up?" Melisa's mom called out.

"Debs, is that you?" Neah's mom asked.

"Yes, it certainly is!" Melisa's mom responded.

The two women ran toward each other and embraced so tightly, not even the air could squeeze between them.

"I can't believe it—long time no see!" Neah's mom said, smiling.

Apparently, the two ladies had worked for the same company a while back before they both relocated to the city.

"So this is your baby?" Neah's mom asked, pointing at Melisa.

"Yes, that's she," Melisa's mom said proudly.

"And this is Neah, my little honey plum," Neah's mom gushed.

"So *this* is the Neah Melisa's been telling me about all semester?" Melisa's mom asked, raising an eyebrow.

"Did you girls know that your moms used to be friends?" she continued. "So you two have no business fighting."

"No, they certainly don't," Neah's mom agreed.

"So, whatever's going on between the both of you, you better fix it before *we* do," Melisa's mom said with a smirk before turning her attention back to Ericka.

"So girl, what have you been up to?" Debbie asked.

"Well, life's been something of a rollercoaster," Ericka replied. "But guess what—that's my favorite ride!"

The two women burst out laughing.

Neah kicked at a pebble near her foot, avoiding Melisa's eyes.

Melisa adjusted the strap of her backpack, clutching the white trash bag that now held most of her school stuff.

"So..." Neah started, her voice barely above a whisper. "That was weird, huh?"

Melisa cracked a small smile.

"Yeah. I didn't even know our moms knew each other like that."

"They were like... full-on hugging. I thought you were gonna cry back there in the classroom or something," Neah said, finally looking at her.

"I actually did," Melisa admitted.

"Yeah, me too—in the hallway." Neah nodded slowly. "I didn't mean for everything to go down like that today."

There was a long pause between them. Neither girl really knew what to say next. The air was filled with the sound of their moms chatting and laughing like old times.

"I guess we both kind of messed up," Melisa finally said.

"Yeah. But maybe we don't have to keep messing up,"

Neah replied. "I mean, if our moms could be friends, I guess we can at least try."

Melisa nodded.

"Deal."

They both stood in silence for a moment.

Then Melisa asked, "Hey, do you still have that necklace from your grandma?"

Neah touched the chain around her neck, surprised she noticed.

"Yeah. I always wear it when stuff gets crazy."

"I think it's cool," Melisa said. "Like your secret superpower or something."

Neah smiled for the first time all day.

"Thanks."

Just then, their moms turned around.

"You girls ready?" Debbie called out.

"Yeah, we're good," Neah said.

As they walked toward the cars, Melisa glanced sideways. "Want to FaceTime later? Maybe start on that science fair reflection thing together?"

"Sure," Neah said. "And possibly, we can work on our math too. You still owe me a rematch from that decimal game.”

Melisa grinned.

“You wish.”

For the first time that day, things didn’t feel so heavy. As the girls climbed into their cars, both moms gave each other a look—one of quiet relief.

Maybe things were going to be okay after all.

Chapter 13

I'm Gonna Be Alright

As Neah said her final goodbyes and headed to her mom's car, she gently searched for her pink and white blanket that she had left in the back seat. She settled into her favorite spot—right behind her mother.

"Okay, Neah, let's get out of here," her mom said.

Neah nodded in response.

"Are you hungry? Do you want something to drink?" her mom asked, glancing back at her momentarily.

"I'm fine for now, Mom," Neah responded.

Soon, her mom rolled out of the school's parking lot.

"We have a lot to talk about, Mama," her mom said gently.

"You do know that you're suspended from school, right?"

"Yes," Neah replied quietly.

"How many times have I told you that fighting doesn't solve anything—except getting you into more trouble?" her mom said, keeping her eyes on the road.

"I know, Mom... but Melisa kept aggravating me, and I just lost it," Neah explained.

"I understand, ma'am. But what could you have done instead of fighting her?" her mom asked.

"Well... I guess I could've told the teacher," Neah admitted.

"But when I tell the teacher, she doesn't really do anything about it. She just takes away Melisa's recess—and honestly, I don't think that's enough. Frankly, I think she needs more punishment for aggravating me. Don't you think?" Neah asked, hoping her mom would take her side.

But her mom shook her head.

"No, Neah. Things don't work like that. If the teacher takes away Melisa's recess, you need to leave it at that. Miss Winters is the teacher—not you."

"Well... I guess I was wrong," Neah whispered.

For the rest of the ride home, Neah sat completely silent. She tucked her head against the window and gazed at the tall pine trees lining the road.

I wish I were as tall and strong as those trees. Then no one would dare mess with me, she thought.

Trees got it so good, and they don't even know it.

- **They're so tall and intimidating.**

- **They don't argue. They don't stress. They just... exist.**

- **They're strong. They don't care what anyone says about them. They're confident in who they are.**

- **They survive the harshest times—winter storms, hurricanes... sure, a few weak ones fall,**

but most? They survive.

Just then, Destiny's Child's *"I'm a Survivor, I'm gonna make it"* began bubbling in her spirit.

Neah pulled out her phone and found the song.

The chorus became her anthem in the back of the car.

"You go, girl! That's the spirit!" her mom chimed in with a smile.

"You're definitely a survivor—and you're definitely gonna make it."

Neah chuckled a little. "Yes, Mom," she said softly.

Soon, her phone lit up. It was Gina.

The text read:

"Are you okay?"

"I miss you."

A smile trickled across Neah's face.

"I miss you already," Neah texted back.

Another message came in:

"Are you home yet?"

"No, Gee Gee. I'm just about turning into the drive-

way," she replied.

"**Alright, I'm gonna FaceTime you over the weekend,**" Gina said.

"**And don't worry about anything. You're my best friend ever.**"

"**Sure thing** " Neah responded, sending her a smiling emoji.

One thing was for sure: **Neah could always count on Gina.**

Even on her saddest days, Gina was that kind of friend—the kind who always showed up.

I mus you
atread!

About the author

Latoya Hewitt Panton is an imaginative storyteller and educator who brings adventure, mystery, and heart to life through her writing. With a passion for inspiring young minds, she created the

series—a thrilling and heartfelt journey that follows a brave young girl named Neah as she navigates challenges, uncovers secrets, and discovers her inner strength. Blending, history, fantasy, and adventure with real-world themes like friendship, courage, and resilience, Latoya's stories captivate readers and spark curiosity. Her work reflects her belief that every child has a spark of greatness just waiting to shine.

Neah's Escape Book #2

In Book 2, Neah is back—and this time, her magical necklace pulls her into a thrilling adventure across the globe! When strange messages lead her to Paris, Neah and her best friend Gina race against time to uncover a hidden secret behind the world's most famous painting—the Mona Lisa. With Gina's magic watch and a mystery that spans centuries, the girls must outsmart ancient clues and dodge danger in the Louvre. Can they unlock the truth before it's too late?

Neah's Escape Book #3

In Book 3, Neah and Gina find themselves trapped in the middle of a terrifying, massive monster invasion. With hope slipping away, Alex arrives just in time—towering above the chaos in his high-tech spacecraft. Together, the three friends fight back against the monstrous threat, using their courage, quick thinking, and a few clever gadgets to survive the attack and protect each other.